PRAISE FOR

A fabulous soaring thriller.

— *Take Over at Midnight,* Midwest Book
Review

Meticulously researched, hard-hitting, and suspenseful.

— *Pure Heat,* Publishers Weekly, starred
review

Expert technical details abound, as do realistic military missions with superb imagery that will have readers feeling as if they are right there in the midst and on the edges of their seats.

— *Light Up the Night,* RT Reviews, 4 1/2 stars

Buchman has catapulted his way to the top tier of my favorite authors.

— Fresh Fiction

Nonstop action that will keep readers on the edge of their seats.

— *Take Over at Midnight,* Library Journal

M L. Buchman's ability to keep the reader right in the middle of the action is amazing.

The only thing you'll ask yourself is, "When does the next one come out?"

The first...of (a) stellar, long-running (military) romantic suspense series.

I knew the books would be good, but I didn't realize how good.

Buchman mixes adrenalin-spiking battles and brusque military jargon with a sensitive approach.

13 times "Top Pick of the Month"

Tom Clancy fans open to a strong female lead will clamor for more.

— *Drone*, Publishers Weekly

Superb! Miranda is utterly compelling!

— *Booklist,* starred review

Miranda Chase continues to astound and charm.

— Barb M.

Escape Rating: A. Five Stars! OMG just start with *Drone* and be prepared for a fantastic binge-read!

— Reading Reality

The best military thriller I've read in a very long time. Love the female characters.

— *Drone,* Sheldon McArthur, founder of The Mystery Bookstore, LA

TO SEE THE MOON

A SECRET SERVICE DOG ROMANCE STORY

M. L. BUCHMAN

SIGN UP FOR M. L. BUCHMAN'S NEWSLETTER TODAY

and receive:
Release News
Free Short Stories
a Free Book

Get your free book today. Do it now.
free-book.mlbuchman.com

Other works by M. L. Buchman: *(* - also in audio)*

Action-Adventure Thrillers

Dead Chef
One Chef!
Two Chef!

Miranda Chase
Drone*
Thunderbolt*
Condor*
Ghostrider*
Raider*
Chinook*
Havoc*
White Top*
Start the Chase*

Science Fiction / Fantasy

Deities Anonymous
Cookbook from Hell: Reheated
Saviors 101

Single Titles
Monk's Maze
the Me and Elsie Chronicles

Contemporary Romance

Eagle Cove
Return to Eagle Cove
Recipe for Eagle Cove
Longing for Eagle Cove
Keepsake for Eagle Cove

Love Abroad
Heart of the Cotswolds: England
Path of Love: Cinque Terre, Italy

Where Dreams
Where Dreams are Born
Where Dreams Reside
Where Dreams Are of Christmas*
Where Dreams Unfold
Where Dreams Are Written
Where Dreams Continue

Non-Fiction

Strategies for Success
Managing Your Inner Artist/Writer
Estate Planning for Authors*
Character Voice
Narrate and Record Your Own
Audiobook*

Short Story Series by M. L. Buchman:

Action-Adventure Thrillers

Dead Chef

Miranda Chase Origin Stories

Romantic Suspense

Antarctic Ice Fliers

US Coast Guard

Contemporary Romance

Eagle Cove

Other

Deities Anonymous (fantasy)

Single Titles

The Emily Beale Universe
(military romantic suspense)

The Night Stalkers
MAIN FLIGHT
The Night Is Mine
I Own the Dawn
Wait Until Dark
Take Over at Midnight
Light Up the Night
Bring On the Dusk
By Break of Day
Target of the Heart
Target Lock on Love
Target of Mine
Target of One's Own
NIGHT STALKER HOLIDAYS
*Daniel's Christmas**
*Frank's Independence Day**
*Peter's Christmas**
Christmas at Steel Beach
*Zachary's Christmas**
*Roy's Independence Day**
*Damien's Christmas**
Christmas at Peleliu Cove

Henderson's Ranch
*Nathan's Big Sky**
*Big Sky, Loyal Heart**
*Big Sky Dog Whisperer**
*Tales of Henderson's Ranch**

Shadow Force: Psi
*At the Slightest Sound**
*At the Quietest Word**
*At the Merest Glance**
*At the Clearest Sensation**

Dilya's Dog Force
(formerly:
White House Protection Force)
*Off the Leash**
*On Your Mark**
*In the Weeds**

Firehawks
Pure Heat
Full Blaze
*Hot Point**
*Flash of Fire**
Wild Fire
SMOKEJUMPERS
*Wildfire at Dawn**
*Wildfire at Larch Creek**
*Wildfire on the Skagit**

Delta Force
*Target Engaged**
*Heart Strike**
*Wild Justice**
*Midnight Trust**

Emily Beale Universe Short Story Series

The Night Stalkers
The Night Stalkers Stories
The Night Stalkers CSAR
The Night Stalkers Wedding Stories
The Future Night Stalkers

Delta Force
Th Delta Force Shooters
The Delta Force Warriors

Firehawks
The Firehawks Lookouts
The Firehawks Hotshots
The Firebirds

Dilya's Dog Force
Stories

Future Night Stalkers
Stories (Science Fiction)

The Emily Beale Universe
Reading Order Road Map

any series and any novel may be read stand-alone
(all have a complete heartwarming happy ever after)

The Emily Beale Universe

- The Night Stalkers #1 *The Night Is Mine*
- The Night Stalkers Stories

- Night Stalker Holidays
- Delta Force
- Firehawks

- Henderson's Ranch
- Delta Force Stories
- Smokejumpers

- Dilya's Dog Force* → DDF Stories
- Fire Lookout Stories

- ShadowForce PSI
- CSAR Stories
- Hotshots Stories

- The Future Night Stalkers
- Firebirds Stories

* *Formerly:* White House Protection Force
For more information and alternate reading orders, please visit:
www.mlbuchman.com/reading-order

ABOUT THIS BOOK

.

W<small>HEN A SMALL DOG MUST SAVE THE DAY, CAN SHE SAVE HER</small> *master's heart as well?*

"I adore the bond between the canine and handler and I can't wait to read about more of these fantastic teams." – Night Owl Reviews Top Pick, Off the Leash

Randi the Corgi lives to sniff out explosives for the US Secret Service. Her final assignment: to protect a major international conference at the historic Mount Washington Hotel.

Dana Meriel Parker may be named after an Irish fairy, but her entire adult life has been working in dangerous locations with Randi. With her sniffer-companion's upcoming retirement, Dana's future lurks as a void filled with fear.

Randall Flynn runs the resort's food services with pride and style, until he trips on a pint-sized sniffer dog. He never believed in the hotel's ghost until he sees the fairy bright Dana Parker. If she's real, can he convince her to stay in his world?

A heart-warming romantic suspense set in the heart of New Hampshire's autumn leaves.

1

"Come here, Randy! Here! Here!"

Randall spun around to see who had the temerity to summon him in such a manner. It was not how he was used to being addressed as the Director of Food Services for the elite Mount Washington Hotel. They were a four-star establishment after all. And were soon headed to a fifth star, and a Michelin Star for their restaurant if he had anything to do with it. And after he achieved that here, he could have his choice of any resort in the world.

He didn't spot anyone seeking his attention in the grand main lobby. It was part of his job to make sure that every patron in any of the hotel's two restaurants, three bars, and room service were always happy. He wasn't above taking an order or clearing a table when needed. But he also was *never* hailed like a busboy still working the Seattle Westin Hotel banquet room. That had been a long grind he'd rather forget forever.

Randall heard the call repeated behind a cluster of Japanese delegates and circled to his right. They'd arrived here in northern New Hampshire two days before the international conference to play golf at the resort's two courses.

The "Here, Randy. Here. Here." was fading as he worked his way around them and entered the body of the main lobby. It stretched half a football field in length from the front desk to the grand ballroom. Its two-plus-story height and fifty-foot width was shifted from vast to merely overwhelming by a long double-row of columns that conducted the patrons to cozy sitting areas scattered throughout.

A tedious party of giggling debutantes fresh from their first ball had shanghaied one long side section, shoving chairs and sofas together like they were in their own dens. Habit had him clearing a half-dozen plates of Lobster en Brioche and trio of chilled jumbo shrimp. All polished clean he was pleased to see.

Their pleasant chatter found the sudden focus of a male, himself, in their presence. He'd normally stop and offer a bit of a flirt. Happy patrons always ordered more.

But the "Randy. Randy." call had moved farther along the hall. He signaled Peter, one of the handsomer bus boys, and suggested that the ladies were running low on snacks, then faded quickly down the hall before they could trap him as well; Peter would not be escaping quickly to place any fresh order. Besides, they were half Randall's age, and while the hotel had many perks, he'd always believed that the female patrons shouldn't be one—no matter what they thought on the matter.

He should be checking in with the Rosebrook Lounge. They were going to be hit hard tonight between the late-departing debutante's parents and the early-arriving conference delegates.

Instead he followed the call past several of the smaller

conference rooms...and the next call came from behind him.

The Mount Washington Hotel was rather famously haunted, but he had certainly never encountered Princess Caroline's ghost. Besides, the ghost generally restricted herself to Suite 314 where she'd lived for decades or the mezzanine overlooking the far end of the vast lobby. And it was late-afternoon, not *spooky* nighttime.

Still, if not Princess Caroline, it was hard not to imagine one of Stephen King's ghosts luring Jack Torrance to madness and rampaging about with an axe.

"Here, Randy! Here! Here!"

Foolishness!

He retraced his steps and heard the call coming from inside the Gold Room. It was the room where in 1944 the US government had rammed the US Dollar down the throats of the forty-three other allies of World War II, replacing the Gold Standard with their own. A superpower in war, the only one still really functioning after the war, the United States made themselves the superpower of the monetary future by linking all of those currencies to the dollar.

He hesitated at the turn into the open door.

What ghost could sound so cheerful calling, "Here, Randy! Here! Here!" in the light tones of New England female?

The westering sunlight shone through the window, making the woman standing before it glow. Her thick dark hair was a brilliant halo that shadowed her face into invisibility. Her trim silhouette appeared to shimmer in the blinding light.

"Are you a ghost?" For once the question didn't sound stupid at all.

2

"Fairy, not ghost. Actually only half fairy. Half goddess too." Dana replied.

The man at the door worked his jaw, but no sound issued forth. If he didn't ask, she wasn't going to explain that Dana Meriel Parker was named for an Irish goddess and a mythological nymph—not technically a fairy but the connotations of nymph in today's world had caused her to shift that.

The sun wasn't low enough to reach him directly, but enough bounced off the polished dark oak of the fourteen-seat round conference table to light him well.

He was definitely a man designed to wear a suit. Not her type, but it looked so very good on him.

Then he yelped, followed closely by a deep complaint of "Tully!" as a Cavalier King Charles Spaniel brushed between his legs. It trotted straight at her passing out of sight under the oak table. No question about where it was headed.

Dana looked down at her own working Corgi and

whispered, "*Maith an cailín!*"—Good girl in Irish—to let her off duty.

On cue, the spaniel emerged from under the table, at least a twitching nose's worth sticking past the edge of a chair.

Then she focused once more on the ever-so-pretty man. He didn't strike her as the yelping type. He was more the type that she wanted to muss his hair and undo his tie to see if he collapsed into a puddle of disarray. Could the man survive such a distasteful dishevelment? By his look, Dana doubted it.

"Who are you talking to?"

"My dog."

"Your dog?" he pushed up on his toes trying to see over the table. Finally he circled around enough to see the two dogs. Randi wore her typical black Kevlar vest with the word *Police* in silver. The spaniel wore its brown-and-white fur.

She eased the lead and her Corgi slipped up nose-to-nose with Tully.

"You're not a ghost." Was he relieved or disappointed?

"I said I wasn't."

"But you were calling me."

"No, *that* must have been a ghost. Just a goddess and fairy remember."

"I remember," he offered her a dazzling smile that said his recovery time was very good. He was also a man used to the godly powers of his looks and his mighty suit. "And yet someone was calling my name."

"No. I was talking to Randi," she nodded down to her Corgi who was now into the butt-sniff thing that dogs so enjoyed.

"I'm Randy."

"That doesn't fit your suit." She knelt down and offered the back of her hand to Tully for consideration.

"Randall, actually. Randall Flynn," he actually straightened the already perfect set of his jacket.

"Oh, so close!" She looked up at him after the spaniel decided it would accept an ear scratch and its bulging eyes, characteristic of the breed, slid half closed.

"So close to what?"

"Why Randi Flagg, of course." Her Corgi looked up at her in surprise and she repeated her *Good girl* command.

"Randi Flagg?" Randall's tone was drier than dog kibble. "Stephen King's Randall Flagg? The villain of *The Stand?*"

"Well, that might be you, but Randi Flagg is my wee devil dog. Her name is pronounced with an *I* because she's a girl." She pointed down to her dog. "You don't pronounce your name with an *I,* do you?" She pointed at him.

"I do not," his indignant tone was about to point out that they sounded exactly the same, but his quirk of a smile said maybe not. "You have a Welsh Corgi named for a Stephen King demon incarnate, who you address in...Irish?"

"She's bilingual, Irish and English." Dana liked that he *hadn't* gone for the obvious. That he'd recognized the language was a pure bonus. Hopefully he didn't also speak it. It might be her heritage but the only part of Irish that she knew was the dog part.

"Here Randi! Here! Here!" He whispered it.

Again her Corgi eyed him strangely.

"It *is* time we returned to our work." She turned from Randall to Randi, "*Amach leat! Out you go!*"

"Work? What work?"

And Randi instantly ignored the Cavalier King Charles Spaniel and waited for her directing command.

Dana tapped the left breast of her vest.

His eyes traveled down for the first time to the logo there.

Before he could begin the whole *A pretty woman like you isn't really a Secret Service agent* thing, she went back to work, guiding Randi around the edges of the room, "*Seo*, Randi. *Seo! Seo!*" And Randi dutifully sniffed each place Dana pointed to as they made sure the room had no hidden explosives.

She risked a glance back as they finished the Gold Room and headed out the door to check the large ballroom that would be used for most of the upcoming meetings.

The Cavalier King Charles Spaniel was looking after his new friend, surprised at his abrupt dismissal.

And the handsome Randall Not-quite-the-demon-Flagg Flynn's expression looked much the same.

3

RANDALL DIDN'T NEED TO SEE THE BLACK T-SHIRT WITH THE large USSS letters across the back. He recognized the Secret Service dog handler by her thick fall of curling black hair the moment he exited the hotel's back door. Beside the long pool, she was stretching out her quads. The predawn light revealed runner's togs rather than a swimsuit. Wise, as the autumn chill was forcing all except the hardiest of souls to the indoor pool. They'd be draining the outdoor pool in the next week or so.

"You would consider going for a run without your faithful companion?" He wasn't sure why he decided to start his greeting with a tease. Maybe hoping to surprise her as much as she'd surprised him.

She barely hesitated in her stretches at his greeting. She certainly didn't turn for him to finally see her face that had been hidden yesterday by the bright sun behind her. Then she'd pointed out the Secret Service logo, making it hard to see anything else.

She switched to the other leg.

"She'd rather sleep in. Randi Flagg may be a devil of a

Corgi, but she's also getting old. This is our last assignment before she retires. Two years of training and eight years of sniffing, that's two more than most dogs last." He noted the pride mixed with the sadness.

Randall began his own warm-up stretches. "I've never seen a pint-sized sniffer dog. Why is the Secret Service checking my hotel for drugs?"

"Randi isn't trained for drugs. Like Randall Flagg's Trashcan Man, she's trained for finding explosives."

"How does she tell you she's found anything?"

"She sits."

"She sits down if she finds explosives? Why the hell doesn't she run away?"

"Because she's been trained to sit."

Randall's brain, which had been terribly pre-occupied by the Secret Service agent since meeting her, hadn't been ready for that. "You look for things that are about to *blow up? And then you *sit there!*" Explosions were supposed to be faced down by big macho guys wearing massive suits in far off war zones.

"We don't exactly hang around afterwards, but yep." She stopped stretching and began a light jog in place. "Though we hope things aren't *about* to blow up. I've had advanced electronics training, but I'd much rather call in a trained EOD specialist."

"EOD?" As if he was supposed to know what that meant.

"Explosive Ordnance Disposal."

And now he wished he still *didn't* know what that meant.

She headed off at a trot.

"Mind if I join you?" Damn it, he wasn't close to stretched out yet. He'd been too busy watching the woman who still hadn't faced him. Then he caught sight of her smile, beneath wrap-around sunglasses, reflected in the still-dark hotel windows.

"If you can keep up." And she was off.

Damn it twice. They hadn't so much as started and he was already behind.

4

_____

DANA DIDN'T SET A HARD PACE TO DUST HIM.

She should.

Mr. Suit, whose deep voice she'd recognized as easily as his reflection, hadn't cared enough to ask her name. And though she'd been able to see him looking at her from behind, he hadn't been checking her out, at least not much. Instead, he'd been having a conversation with the back of her head.

But she didn't dust him. Instead she stayed at a warm-up pace as he caught up and ran beside her.

"Goddess and fairy?" As if they'd done it a hundred times before, they circled the north end of the hotel, picked up Base Station Road, and turned right. Today was a good day for distance, so she'd planned a road run. Besides, Mr. Suit, no matter how fine he looked in running shorts and his hundred-dollar high-tech shirt, didn't look like any kind of a trail runner.

"Yep!" No way was she going to make it easy for him. The morning was unusually warm for late September in the White Mountains of New Hampshire, which meant she should have started with a light jacket over her Secret Service long-sleeved t-shirt. But she hadn't and was glad for even the thin coverage of her goose-bumped arms.

As soon as they were clear of the resort, the road plunged into the trees. The maples had gone dark red and the birches sparkling gold. The oaks were indecisive and had mostly settled for a consensus in the oranges. The elms' contributions were already shuffling beneath their feet in lazy swirls of brown.

Poking up above the trees, punching their white tops into the crystalline blue sky, the Presidentials were already snow-capped. Adams, Jefferson, and Washington peaks would honor that White Mountains name for the next eight or nine months before they melted bare again. Her youth had started in St. Johnsbury at the west end of the Whites and finished in Boston. It was decidedly strange to be so close to her parents' place again.

"I've never met a goddess, nor a fairy for that matter, walking our mere mortal earth." He was enjoying the game she'd set up rather than asking, *Hey, what's your name, babe.* She definitely liked that.

"You still haven't. We're running."

"True. I do meet them a thousand times more often when I'm running."

"A thousand...times zero."

His laugh confirmed his victory of that round. Or maybe he simply appreciated someone understanding his joke in turn.

"Dana, from Danann or Danu, the Irish mother goddess. Meriel, Irish for sea nymph. And Parker for great-great-granddda who crossed the Irish Sea from the heathen land of England, and lies buried in a proper Irish graveyard." And the generation before hers was never to be mentioned and best forgotten—a trick she still hadn't mastered.

"None of which are fairies. You're a goddess and nymph." Randall hesitated, actually bobbling a step in what had been a very smooth run up to that moment. "Uh, right. That didn't come out right. I see why you chose fairy heritage over nymph heritage."

"No," because Randall was too fun to tease and she couldn't let him off the hook with the obvious. "I claim fairy heritage because I have a Pembroke Welsh Corgi as a companion."

"You mean a familiar?"

"There's no such thing as witches."

"But there are goddesses and fairies?"

"Of course there are, Randall Flynn. I'm Irish after all."

"Plus a sixteenth English."

"Blaggard. Troll." She stretched out her stride, and he matched her easily. They were approaching a Y in the road, and Randall must have noticed her uncertainty.

"Shorter," he pointed left. "Though a nice set of waterfalls." Then he pointed right. "Longer, more elevation. Another set of falls and the cog railway up the mountain."

She went right. The two-lane road, which had been playing games with the Ammonoosuc River, now settled in to follow the curving canyon the water had dug over the centuries. It slewed and burbled over rounded rocks alongside, making it the perfect fall dawn. The road bent right and mostly leveled out as it followed the contour lines.

"Welsh Corgi," he succinctly placed his marker in the conversation without making it sound as if he was short of breath.

"Next time you see Randi, when she's not wearing her Kevlar work vest, take a good look at her coat. You can clearly see the darker markings of the saddle from when the fairies used to ride them to battle."

"So you ride your Corgi?"

"At least in a sense—sense of smell that is. I couldn't do what I do without her sensitive nose."

"Dana Meriel Parker and her Corgi Randi Flagg. Goddess, nymph, one-sixteenth heathen, fairy, demon. That's quite a set of skills you bring to the game."

"You ain't seen nothing yet." And she stretched out her stride to the next-level ground-covering gait trained deep into any Secret Service agent.

She wasn't gasping, but she had no extra air to waste on conversation either. Side-by-side they continued upward. Across a small bridge over the rushing river, that she'd have to come back and admire some other time, the road began to climb in earnest. A glance at her workout watch showed a four-hundred-foot elevation gain in the first six kilometers.

The last two climbed twice that.

5

Why? Why? Why?

Maybe some ghost had it in for him and *made* him turn it into a race. He'd tried to outrun a US Secret Service agent. *What* had he been thinking?

Randall staggered into the main lobby after a shower, walking on Jell-O legs. He straightened his suit jacket, took a deep breath...and it didn't help at all.

And there was Princess Caroline's portrait gazing sardonically down at him from the mezzanine. Her husband had died shortly after opening the hotel, and five years later she'd married a French prince. Despite that, and her subsequent purchase of several European hotels, she'd spent most of her life living in and overseeing her first love, the Mount Washington Hotel.

The Princess had *always* been the best dressed at dinner. She'd done that by hovering invisibly behind a sheer curtain on the mezzanine and watching all the ladies going in to dinner. Then she chose her attire to outshine them all, arriving fashionably late. Now her more than life-size portrait lurked there, observing his dismal failure.

He'd matched Dana all the way up to the Cog Railway's base station that climbed to the top of Mount Washington in fairer weather—even if she did run like a goddess. But on the eight-kilometer descent, she had floated like a fairy incarnate. As his normal, ha, *ever* run limit was 10K, by kilometer twelve he'd waved her ahead. By thirteen she was long gone and by sixteen he'd been staggering.

And now Princess Caroline's ghost, or at least her portrait, was considering him with disdain.

For thinking he could keep up with Agent Dana Parker?

Or for thinking that he'd ever walk normally again?

"Are you okay?" Dana was at his elbow, neatly dressed in black slacks, white shirt, and black Secret Service vest. Randi plumped down onto her butt, but she was apparently in *normal dog* mode as his shoe didn't immediately explode. In fact, Randi with an *I* was ignoring his shoe completely and instead watching Tully as the Cavalier King Charles Spaniel came trotting over from the front desk where he often worked the welcoming line.

"Don't I look okay?" Or maybe he wasn't. It was the first time he'd seen her eyes and they were as blue as her hair was black. They were both warm with concern and startling with the color of the summer sky.

"You look as if you've ridden a horse for the first time in your life," Dana's laugh was soft but it seemed to light a hint of a smile on the Princess' portrait gazing down at them.

He turned his back on the Princess, then hoped that he hadn't just offended her ghost. Word was that Princess Caroline could be very tricky. "My morning runs are more normally a 5K. I'll occasionally do a 10K. Today…"

"Sixteen. You were being an idiot," then she grimaced at her own words.

But that didn't stop her lecture, which was another thing

to like about her. His siblings had been all about coy digs and passive-aggressive triumphs. His parents cared more about their work than their children. He'd strived to be just like them. It was easier, safer.

Dana was more the forthright battering ram type.

"You're lucky you didn't hurt yourself, Randall. Especially after a short warm-up. And did you not turn back because you were competing with me? Or were you chasing after me?"

He sighed as he looked into Dana's wondrous eyes. "Yes." *To both.*

"Hmm…" she made it a thoughtful sound. Then she straightened his tie. "Man looks good running *and* good in a suit."

Then she squatted as if she hadn't run sixteen kilometers this morning, or even one, played with Tully for a moment, then shooed him off toward his front desk duties.

"I'm supposed to redo the conference spaces and then tour the shops, indoor pool, and fitness area along Stickney Street downstairs. After lunch, I'm scheduled to be doing your domain of the dining and kitchen areas."

"Meet me for lunch in The Cave and we can lay out a plan."

"Still chasing me Randall Not-quite-Flagg?"

"Is it working?" He hadn't chased after a woman in a while. He shouldn't now as she'd be gone at the end of the upcoming conference…but he wanted to.

"Ask me over lunch." Then she commanded her dog's attention and departed leaving behind a soft, "Here, Randi! Here! Here!"

6

After giving Randi a pee break and a chance to sit in the late morning sun to warm herself, Dana led her to The Cave. A hidden speakeasy during Prohibition, it was now a fancy bar.

Through a brickwork arch, a narrow stone-lined corridor lit by scattered twinkle lights led deep under the hotel. It opened into a cozy bar filled with intimate scattered tables, mostly for two she noted, and a big wooden service bar. The walls were heavy stone and the low-beamed ceiling dark wood.

She and Randi stood at the threshold as their eyes adapted to the dim lighting.

"Agent Parker?" The bartender addressed her. He continued at her nod, "Mr. Flynn is briefly delayed and asked me to make sure you were settled. Can I get you anything while you wait?"

"Lemonade and a bowl of water."

He didn't blink at the second request, simply guiding her to a corner table where he whisked away a small *Reserved* sign as if he knew she'd want her back to two walls. She was a sniffer dog handler, not a protection detail field agent but she'd been through enough training scenarios to prefer the corner.

Randall arrived only moments behind the drinks. "I thought you'd appreciate the corner table."

"I do." So *he* was the one being considerate. He kept exceeding her expectations. "What made you think of it?"

Randall smiled as he sat beside her. "I've been working the hotel food trade since I was born. My parents worked at a place in Seattle called the Edgewater Inn, perched on the scenic waterfront. I started off in their footsteps, busboy, waiter, and finally cook. At which point I discovered that I'm a good cook but I'm no chef."

"I can make cereal, does that count?"

He shook his head sadly but smiled. "Not unless you open the box yourself."

"Easy." She swung her wrist down and her Benchmade knife dropped out of its forearm holster and dropped into her hand. With a flick she snapped it open.

Rather than looking alarmed, Randall simply nodded, "Yes, I expect that would suffice."

She pondered why she'd done that as she closed and slid the knife away. To spook him or impress him? And why would she want to do either one? He certainly hadn't responded in either of those ways. Instead he kept that perfect equanimity that had only broken at their very first meeting when Tully had brushed against his leg unexpectedly while he was thinking she was a ghost.

Dana took a small bet with herself that it would be truly interesting to discover what he kept so carefully behind that wall. It was the sort of bet she never told to others or acted on, but she'd still bet it would be interesting to find out.

"You were telling me you were no chef."

"Yes. But I *was* fascinated by how each of the hotels I worked at functioned. From chef I went to *maître d'*. From there I jumped over to management of both front and back of house. Now, I'm the *maître d'hôtel* and I oversee all food services at one of the top six ski resorts in all of North America, including Canada. We're Number One in the East. I've only been here seven months and three days, but I think we might rate top five this year. Comes off the tongue much better, doesn't it? And I'm working to make us a destination for more than skiing and hiking, but also for food. From here? Well, I don't know what's next. Speaking of which, that's far too much about me and we should order."

He barely lifted a finger and a waitress teleported into place.

Dana had been distracted by Randall's story. He'd worked incredibly hard to become what he was; at least as hard as she'd worked to become a Secret Service agent. For two such disparate professions, that was an interesting connection.

She gazed down at the bar menu, which was thankfully short...and expensive. If she paid for this lunch and ate her grocery-store sandwich for dinner, her per diem would cover most of the expense. When working resorts, the agents typically ate in a nearby town—which here meant Munroe's Family Restaurant that she'd already scoped out five miles to the west.

"Two of the Old School Pressed Burgers. One with all of the trimmings and one with none of them, just the meat for my dog. Mine cooked medium, hers very rare."

The waitress nodded without hesitation and turned to Randall.

"That sounds good, but without the dog's portion."

And she evaporated with the perfect service that barely impinged on Dana's awareness.

"I expected you to eat something..." And she shut her mouth to avoid being ruder than her norm.

"More froufrou?" Randall laughed. "I assure you, that is not me."

"Despite the suit."

He looked down at his clothes. "Despite the suit."

Now that was intriguing.

7

RANDALL HAD USED DANA'S INVESTIGATION OF HIS DOMAIN AS an excuse to stay near her. But when she and Randi were working, she was oblivious to everything else around her.

Except she wasn't. Anyone within a certain range was *completely* on her radar. He'd quickly learned her awareness boundary and worked to stay out of it to avoid distracting her. Only moving in when she gave him a *Where next?* look.

It did afford him time to meet with each and every team member throughout the vast complex while she and her dog checked out every corner and drawer of every room. He liked the floor managing style.

The hotel was gearing up for a major conference. The last of the debutantes were gone and the Secret Service now had greeting teams that vetted every new arrival at the hotel. They were stationed in vehicles along the entry drive, and at the lobby entrance.

Perimeter security at each entrance checked every person who returned from a trail hike or the golf course. More patrolled the outer perimeter.

Randall doubted if the resort had ever been locked

down this hard. The 1944 conference had undoubtedly been secured by the Secret Service, but that had been a different, quieter era. They'd had to keep out foreign spies, not domestic terrorists and the foil-hat conspiracy people.

The hotel manager was going quietly insane trying to keep up with the security arrangements on top of everything else. Dana had only been the prep team, and nothing had prepared them for the massive influx of security.

Three more dogs had joined the patrols, all far bigger and scarier looking than the little Corgi, but they treated Dana and Randi with immense respect.

When he had casually asked, one of them mumbled something about *Not messing with the A-team.*

She was as high in her profession as he was in his. That wasn't something he ran into very often in attractive single women.

Attractive single women? What was he thinking? She'd be gone in three days. She wasn't the sort of woman flings were made for. In fact, she was the sort that—

"Are you done staring?" Dana stood square in front of him without him noticing her arrive there. She was carrying her Corgi.

"Sure you aren't a ghost?" He was in the main kitchen with his butt against the side of one of the twelve-burner stoves, early dinner prep warm against his back.

The team of chefs was on the hustle. With all two hundred rooms at the main hotel booked as well as the hundred and fifty others at the outlying properties and townhouses, they were going to be pushed to their limits. He'd added staff from every corner he could find them, and still it would be a Herculean task by the time they were done.

Oddly, his own duties were running normally. His panic had been spread over the three prior months since the moment the contract was signed for The Second Bretton Woods Financial Conference.

"Not ghost. Goddess and fairy," but her delayed response was not much over a mumble and was accompanied by a tonsil-revealing yawn. "One in need of a hot bath and then we both need to lie down. Too bad my hotel room only has a shower." She was weaving with exhaustion and Randi was already asleep in her arms.

"You're welcome to use mine." His job made him one of the few who were entitled to a permanent room at the hotel.

"The bath and the bed?" She asked the question straight and it was as she did so that the dual meaning sunk in.

"Uh, yes." After the morning run and an entire afternoon of watching her work, he didn't think that he'd ever been so impressed by any woman. "Definitely. For as long as you need to. I have a couch I can stretch out on," he temporized. Though the image of her in his bed could grow on him very rapidly.

She watched him for a long moment, her face unreadable. Long enough that a sous-chef had to nudge him aside so that he could fire off the two burners on the stove that were closest to his butt.

"I'd like that." Her voice was as soft as her hair appeared.

———

RANDALL HAD ORDERED A ROOM SERVICE DINNER—LOBSTER Pot Pie, Black Garlic Braised Beef Rib, and a Beef Tartare without the seasoning for Randi. He ordered in only rarely and he spent the entire time awaiting delivery trying not to think about the woman in his bathtub. In the middle of their dinner, he was called away. He told her to finish and he'd return as quickly as he could—hopefully before she left.

But he was delayed one way and another, and didn't make it back until past eleven. A sixteen-hour day was one of the reasons he'd been given an on-site room. Such days weren't the norm, but they happened.

The heavy drapes were open and the moon was reflecting off Mount Washington's snowy top well enough for him to see his way. He was reaching for the light, assuming Dana was long gone, when he noticed the dark area on the pillows—an area the size of a cloud of hair.

Dana was in his bed. He turned for the couch.

There, nestled in a curl of blankets, her dog snored quietly. That's where *he* was supposed to sleep.

Then he saw the triangular field of white on the bed. She'd folded back the blankets and the sheet on his side. An invitation.

He listened to the night for a long time, gauging his degree of exhaustion and temerity.

The fairy whisper in the night asked, "Are you going to stand there and think, or are you coming to bed?"

"We've known each other for only—"

"I've watched you as long and closely as you watched me. I watched how much people like and respect you. You are a very attractive man, Randall, in many ways. I'm not whimsical but neither am I puritanical. I'm not a—" her voice strangled briefly as she cut herself off then tried again. "I am not like my parents, yet I choose to be here. What do you choose?"

Randall undid his tie, and didn't complain when a fairy-nymph-goddess rose from his bed, naked in the moonlight, to help him out of his suit.

8

"*I'm not like my parents...*" Randall's voice was soft, kind, and Dana would rather wake up in a cat litter box than curled against his shoulder with that question as a greeting.

She considered pushing away, hard—with an elbow to his solar plexus.

Sensing something was wrong, Randall eased his arm where it had been wrapped tight about her shoulders. If he hadn't, she'd have gone. But the thoughtfulness kept her in place.

She turned her face into his shoulder, "Do I really have to explain that?"

"I was more mulling over the words than asking. My parents never aspired to more than the little hotel they ran: restaurant, bar, and room service. It was certainly more important than their kids. They never even become hotel managers; they only cared about the food. I've always sort of looked down on that. As if the deficiency was with them."

Dana lay quietly and listened.

"Rather than a lack of aspiration, I was wondering if

they haven't simply found contentment. I'll have to ask them someday."

"You talk to your parents?" And she felt foolish for asking.

Randall turned to look at her, which was impossible in their present positions, but it placed his face in her hair. Last night he'd proven his fascination with her hair, among many other parts of her body, but especially her *fairy* hair.

"I don't," she answered his unspoken question.

He held her tighter.

"At about eight or nine, I decided that with parents like mine that I had no past, only a future. At fifteen I finally found the nerve and ran away from home. Finished high school from a kid's shelter. Earned money as a dog walker. Made *myself* who I am."

Randall started some pleasant compliment until she freed a hand and rested her fingers over his lips.

"Randi is done when this conference is done. What comes after that for me? I have no idea and it's almost as scary as that fifteen-year-old standing out in the autumn rain. I didn't even have the common sense to run away from home during the summer."

"What do you mean *done?* You'll be assigned another dog and—"

"No. In the Secret Service an agent gets one dog. When the dog retires, the agent is assigned elsewhere. The only thing I was ever good at were the dogs. Certainly never the people the way you are. I saw you yesterday, making every one of your staff feel important."

"They *are* important. And certainly you'll make new friends wherever—"

"False assumption. You think I have friends now. I don't."

"Are you ever going to let me finish a sentence?" Randall complained.

"One in three. That's your limit."

He laughed into her hair and it was a good feeling.

9

RATHER THAN START HIS DAY WITH A JOG, OR AN ATTEMPT TO run with Dana (who insisted he had no bad habits as a runner and was trainable for longer distances), it began with a romp between the sheets. It was a first for him in his hotel room though he'd been here for seven months, but Dana made it worth the wait.

When they showered together, her black hair turned to liquid midnight in the water.

It was a good morning, the best he'd had in a long time, but there was a somberness too. He didn't feel as if he was wearing a goofy grin, knowing this was but a brief moment in time which he surprisingly wanted to be much more. And Dana was fast switching over to all business, he could see her burying her fears of the future under a thick layer of hard-armored professionalism.

The heads of state had started rolling in last night which was what had kept him out late. The Koreans wanted their own food (actually, locating a supply of kimchi had been sufficient), the Japanese were more open to suggestions but wished for lighter fare (meaning they wanted precisely their own cuisine), no one had warned him that half of the Indian delegation and most of the Southeast Asians were vegetarian, though he should have guessed (he and the head chef had rapidly expanded the menu offerings), along with three Danish vegans (one with an intense series of food allergies), and...

Northern New Hampshire wasn't exactly the hotbed of international cuisine, nor stores to buy the ingredients. But with a little creativity they were managing.

Dana took Randi over to play with Tully for a moment.

When he turned from watching them, a tall teen with olive skin, hair that fell in long brown ruffles down to her elbows, and the greenest eyes he'd ever seen planted herself in front of him. At her side sat a fluffy Sheltie.

"What do you think, Zackie?" the teen asked the dog without looking away from Randall's face.

The dog tipped its head as if uncertain.

"Can I help you, Miss?"

"Unlikely," she continued studying him.

"It's my job to—"

"Bed every Secret Service dog handler?" She cut him off.

"What is it with women not letting me finish my sentences today?"

"Hmmm," the girl tipped her head much like the dog's. "Maybe he has possibilities."

"I'm not standing here in the third person either." Then he clamped down on his tongue. He never, ever talked back to a patron, no matter how richly they deserved it. He'd broken up drunken brawls in two-star restaurants and averted murder when two women discovered they were both married to the same man in a biker bar. He was always the calm center, but something about this girl made him all bristly.

"Hi, Dilya." Dana and Randi returned. "What are you doing here?"

The two dogs greeted each other like old friends.

"I hitched a ride."

Dana laughed. "Can't keep a good girl down."

Dilya then turned on an impish grin. "Can't keep a good *woman* down. I'm turning twenty soon. I'm definitely a woman now, aren't I?"

"Absolutely!"

Randall felt like a ping pong ball as the two women went back and forth.

"You're not a Secret Service agent too, are you?" It was hard enough remembering that about Dana because she was so unexpected. But this young...woman?

"No," and she turned back to Dana but he could feel the smirk mocking him even through the fall of hair hiding her face.

"Ha. Ha. Ha."

One eye peered out of the hair and looked up at him. "Oh, Dana. I like him. You should keep him around. Whups! Gotta go!"

She flashed a hand signal to the dog who immediately took off running. Then she sprinted after, calling out in a tone that didn't sound at all upset, "Wait, Zackie. Come back."

Dana was laughing as she bumped a shoulder against his.

"Okay, I give. What's the joke?"

"That's Dilya Stevens, the First Nanny. She started with President Matthews and now works for President Thomas. As a side hobby, she's trained the First Dog meticulously to hand and voice signals."

"But the dog ignored her commands."

"No," Dana flicked her hand a certain way after shielding it from her own dog. "That sent Zackie running into the middle of whatever caught Dilya's attention. So she was *forced* to follow, calling out commands that aren't quite in Zackie's vocabulary. *Wait. Come back.* But not, *No. Stay. Come here. Heel.* The dog is taking her exactly where she wants to go but probably has no right to be." Her target appeared to be, Randall couldn't help gawking, the Prime Minister of the UK and the French President currently in a heated discussion.

"That means—"

"Her clearance is Top Secret or better as are both of her parents. She doesn't share much, except maybe with the President, but she loves knowing everything."

He gazed after the girl trying to imagine her as part of the First Family. "The President. Like *our* President. Hitched a ride with him?"

"The Beast to Air Force One to Marine One. She and that dog nose their way into everywhere. I'd better get started. Thanks for last night and this—"

"Wait a sec," he finally had the chance to cut *her* off. "Do not be saying things like that, I enjoyed it every bit as much as you did. Here." He held out a card.

"What's that?"

"What does it look like? It's a spare key to my room. It's yours for as long as you want it. A day. A week. Whatever."

"I'm only here three more days. Two now." Dana looked down, her voice sad.

He nudged her chin up until he could see her perfect blue eyes, then brushed back her fairy dark hair. "Don't think about that. Think about today. We're both going to be busy, but if we somehow end up in that bed together again, it will have been a good day. Alright?"

She managed a smile and a nod. Then she gave that same hand sign to Randi and she and the dog headed off to work.

"See, I told you," Dilya's voice sounded close by his elbow.

"Aw, give me a break, kid."

Then he looked around and saw the black woman standing beside Dilya. She had a streak of gray in her hair, was strongly built, and formidable. Black eyes and a grim expression that said she was seriously dangerous, and her jacket was open enough to reveal the two sidearms in shoulder holsters.

"We'll see." The woman studied him long enough that he knew she'd be aware of his every movement throughout the rest of the conference. Then she twisted on her heel and stalked off toward the former President who was now the Secretary of State just arriving on the far side of the lobby.

And he'd thought Dana was surprising? He'd stepped into some crazy fairy kingdom and wondered if he'd ever get out again. Or if he wanted to.

10

DANA NEVER CRIED. SHE'D LEFT THAT ON THE DOORSTEPS OF her parents and multiple stepparents on both sides with all of their alcohol, drugs, and sordid affairs.

We're only casual users, dear. Like because they were trust fund babies wealthy enough to buy whatever drugs they wanted, they could destroy themselves and their daughter. *We don't have to care what other people think.* Because they had no morals at all. *We...*

But it almost came out all over Randall's chest on the last morning of the conference. By nightfall, all of the heads of state and delegates would be gone. By dawn, the Secret Service teams would be finished and returning to Washington, DC. And then she and Randi would have finished their years as a team. At least they would let her keep Randi. They'd lived together for too long and it would be cruel to let anyone else adopt the dog.

And she was leaving Randall.

In so few days he had become impossibly important to her. They'd both, all three of them with Randi, worked to exhaustion every day. But the moments they'd had together had been all the more precious.

They hadn't returned to the lovely fall woods though they shimmered out Randall's window like an invitation. And the towering pinnacle of Mount Washington punched into the sky. Whether sunlit against blue or moonlit against black it stood strong and powerful like a promise of so much more.

So much that she'd never dared to reach for.

While he slept, Dana slid out of Randall's bed.

Coaxing Randi awake, they slipped out of the room. They walked together out on the back lawn while the mountain shifted in spirit. With the moon set and the stars going dull with the dawn, the peak almost disappeared.

Then, as the pink brushed the sky, the color was reflected off the snow as if the everchanging mountain was more of the sky than the sky itself. And finally, snatching the first bolt of fire from the sun, it lit like a torch to announce a new day.

Her last day here.

Her last day working with Randi.

Her last day with Randall Flynn.

And she was ready to weep all over again.

She needed to move. To run. To escape who she was being, as she so often did. That was how she'd learned to cover the miles, far more than any Secret Service required standard. Running *from* herself, but since when was that news.

She'd put on her running clothes, but she also had Randi. Taking her dog back to the room might wake Randall. And he was so aware, so kind, that he'd see the utter misery on her face and ask again what she was thinking. Dana doubted if it was in her to refuse him yet one more time.

The fitness studio. The hotel had a whole room of elite gym machines. Randi could nap and she'd get in a quick run on a treadmill.

She took one last look behind her at the sun lighting more and more of the mountain. Dana turned and hurried inside. Soon the light would reach the magic of the leaves and she'd remember the freedom and beauty of that first run through the autumn woods. If she saw that, her next stop would be under Randall's covers and she'd never ever come out again.

In the empty fitness studio, she made a nest for Randi with her sweatshirt, chose a machine, and began to run.

11

When Randall woke alone, he knew something was wrong.

Dana wasn't with him. But there wasn't any feeling of hurt or loss at her silent departure. He'd seen the pain that she tried so hard to hide. That, and he knew he was running out of time.

He figured there were two options. He could enjoy what final minutes they could grab today and call it a wonderful fling.

"Screw that shit," he told the bathroom mirror before he was half shaved.

He dropped his razor in the charger and hurried to fetch his jacket.

Then he hurried once more to the mirror, managed a crap job on the other half of his face, called that good enough, and accidentally dropped the razor in the toilet instead of the charger.

He fished it out, washed it and his arm in soap and hot water, then rushed out to get dressed.

Randall was out in the hallway and down to the third floor by the time he realized that he was still clutching his razor. He stuffed it into a suit jacket pocket where it made an ugly bulge and began dribbling water from inside its mechanism.

He yanked it out and chucked it down a handy garbage chute. Only after he threw it away did he remember that it was waterproof specifically for cleaning.

Screw it.

He continued down to the lowest level.

Except he had dead-ended himself.

The stairs he'd taken were fine down to the main floor. But at the Stickney Street level, which was half underground, they led into a maze. The stairs ended in a small hall. Straight ahead was the wall on the backside of a storeroom.

He'd have to circle all of the way around the end of the building to reach the Garden Corridor, which then led into the heart of his world at the far end of the hotel. He'd start scouting for her there.

The Garden Corridor wrapped around the fitness studio and the indoor pool.

He broke into a run—and almost missed her.

Someone in the fitness studio, at this early hour, was running one of the machines at a high whine. He glanced inside while still on the move—and lambasted himself into the corridor wall getting white cement powder all down the side of his dark suit.

There she was. The treadmill was cranked up to a high speed at a steep angle of attack.

And Dana was sprinting up the slope with all the effortlessness she'd shown running that first day. The woman was goddamn magnificent.

When he opened the door, he whapped Randi where she'd been napping by the threshold. The force of his arrival rolled her over, completely enveloping her in Dana's sweatshirt.

Dana yanked the emergency cord on the treadmill and was dripping sweat on her dog within seconds as she helped Randi get unsnarled.

"You okay, girl? You okay?"

Randi was smiling up at her.

Randall knelt down beside them to check the dog himself because Dana's hands were shaking so badly. That's when he noticed that not all the water was coming from her forehead. It was also dribbling out of her eyes and trickling down off her chin.

He focused on the Corgi. She didn't complain once as he flexed and squeezed each paw, rubbed on ribs, and even tugged on an ear before tickling her nose.

Then he gathered up Dana's hands from where they were buried in the dog's fur.

"She's okay, Dana. Randi is okay."

Dana nodded without speaking.

And without stopping her crying.

When he squeezed her hands tighter she pulled away—which felt like she'd just driven a knife into his heart.

She brushed a hand on his cheek which helped ease the rejection. "Just...give me a minute." And she pushed to her feet and headed for the locker rooms.

Randi looked up at him in question.

Randall waved for her to follow Dana.

He listened to the bright click of claws as the dog left the fitness studio and crossed the cool tile floor of the indoor pool to the locker rooms.

There was a pause.

Then a very, very emphatic curse.

Randall pushed to his feet and raced after the dog.

12

"REALLY?" DANA LOOKED DOWN AT RANDI.

Randall came rushing into the locker room but she put up a hand to stop him where he was.

"What?"

She nodded down to her dog.

He looked down as well. "She's just sitting."

"That's what she does when—" And he must have remembered, because he too cursed emphatically.

Sitting was Randi's signal that she'd found explosives.

13

"GET MY SWEATSHIRT."

Randall wanted to ask why, but one look at her face was sufficient and he bolted back to the fitness studio.

When he returned, she again raised that imperious hand to stop him at the threshold. She crossed to him, and pulled a radio out of the sweatshirt's pocket.

"Beat, Dana here. Randi has a possible positive on the ground floor in the women's locker room off the pool."

He recognized the voice that responded. It was the woman who'd stood beside Dilya yesterday.

"Men's," Randall corrected her.

She looked around in surprise, and must have spotted the line of urinals. "Correction, *men's* locker room. Get me an EOD team and clear the ballroom. We're directly underneath."

She'd been so upset that she hadn't noticed which locker room she was in but she remembered the layout of the labyrinthine hotel without an eyeblink. Damn but she was amazing.

"Whose locker is this?" Dana was still all business.

Randall scanned the line and tried to picture it. His own permanent locker was five down the row. "Uh, Ray Charles."

"He's dead." She was so deadpan that it took him a moment to realize she was joking.

"Not the blind black musician. The hotel's activities and athletics director."

"I didn't meet him."

Randall closed his eyes for a moment. "Uh, six-two, white, ex-military type, medium brown hair—"

Dana was echoing his description over the radio.

He didn't know what else to say. They sat in staff meetings together but had very little to do with each other beyond picnic box lunches for off-site activities like trail rides.

Randall was trying to come up with something else when he was nearly blasted aside.

A three-man team hustled in toting bags of heavy gear.

"You need to go, Randall." Dana was looking at him as they rapidly set up equipment around the locker Randi still sat in front of.

"You, too."

"You aren't trained for this and you don't have protection."

He was about to protest that she didn't either as one of the new arrivals dug out a heavy vest and a helmet with a face shield which Dana donned with quick, practiced moves.

He faded back until he was outside Dana's awareness perimeter.

One of the techs pulled out a fiber optic camera and slithered it into the locker's vents.

"Go!" she said without turning away from the display screen.

Okay, not outside her awareness.

14

DANA WATCHED AS THEY VERIFIED THERE WERE NO BOOBY traps on the locker. She served as the EOD team's communications link, so that they weren't distracted by any outside chatter.

"Locker appears clean."

Beat acknowledged, "We've emptied the ballroom and are sweeping the hotel rooms on the three stories above. Almost everyone is in the Main Dining Room for breakfast." That was good, they were at the far end of the building, a football field away.

The EODs eased open the locker a half-inch and checked everything again while Dana kept Randi clutched tight to her chest. There was a collective sigh of relief when they swung the door wide.

"Hope you were wrong about this one," she whispered to her dog who nuzzled her.

Rather than moving any of the clothes in the locker, one of the techs pulled on nitrile gloves and swabbed the inside of the door and various other metal surfaces, then put the swipe cloth into the trace detector. They all counted out the eight agonizingly long seconds together like a soft mantra.

"Positive," the operator announced as he leaned over the screen.

Dana felt sick, as she did the four other times Randi had found *live* results. Many dogs did an entire career without ever finding explosives off the training range.

"Conventional C-4. And ammonium perchlorate."

One of the other techs shone a flashlight into the locker. "I'm seeing flecks on the cuffs of the sweatshirt that could be powdered aluminum."

She reported the findings to Beat.

"Which means what in English, Dana?"

"Rocket fuel. The C-4 would probably be a trigger. The other two made up the fuel for the Space Shuttle's solid rocket boosters."

"The one that blew up Challenger? Shit!" Beatrice Ann Belfour wasn't much given to swearing.

"And launched more than a hundred others all the way into space. All we have right now are traces." She watched the techs carefully lifting out the clothes, but there simply wasn't anything there.

"And your dog didn't pick it up anywhere else?"

That rocked Dana back on her heels. She and Randi had been over *every inch* of the building for two days before the conference and three more since. She'd known Randall for less than a week—she shoved that thought aside, though it didn't want to go she forced it out.

"How did you not smell this?" she asked Randi.

The dog looked at her as if she was shocked that anything could pass her notice. Which was true. She might be small, but her tests were always at the top of the rankings.

Dana paced away to think while the team finished up with the locker.

Out of the men's locker room, across the joined entry into the pool area, and over into the women's locker. Then back the other way.

She finally stopped in the gap, staring at the indoor pool. Fifty feet long and twenty wide, its surface was lightly rippled by the water circulation jets. At the bottom of the pool was a line of scuba tanks from some recent dive training class. Lounge chairs were circled tastefully around the wide perimeter. Foam float toys for kids in a neat wire bin. A hot tub plunge pool steamed lazily in the corner. Two stately rows of columns down either side supported the massive beams above.

She looked up at the underside of the ballroom floor where the last day's meetings were supposed to begin—she checked her watch—in five minutes.

She looked back down at the pool directly beneath the ballroom.

"Why couldn't you smell it, Randi?" Her dog looked at her. "Because...ammonium perchlorate dissolves in water. Any that had been dusted on along the outside of the scuba tanks is gone."

Dana yelled for the EOD techs and they came running.

"The scuba tanks! They're the bombs."

When she pointed at the line of tanks at the bottom of the pool, one of techs dumped his helmet as he turned his run into a dive.

For thirty long seconds she, the two other techs, and Randi stood and watched.

When he finally surfaced, he shook his head. His grim expression told the rest of the story.

"Evacuate, Beat. Evacuate the building, starting at the South End. This is top priority. This is not a drill."

The tech flashed up five fingers.

"You have five minutes. We'll try to disarm for three minutes but it looks unlikely."

"Roger." Beat's voice was dead calm because nothing flustered the woman.

"Pro job," the tech said as he crawled out of the water. "I touch any tank and the rest of them blow. Half-hour minimum to defuse, if we had air to breathe. Double check me."

The other two techs plunged into the water.

The wait was longer this time, closer to a minute before they both surfaced and gasped for air.

The team leader slashed a flat hand toward the door before he was out of the water.

Simple message, *Run!*

15

RANDALL HAD BEEN WATCHING THROUGH THE CORRIDOR window beyond the far end of the pool when the two technicians emerged from the water like they'd been catapulted.

They sprinted out into the corridor and he met them there.

"Goddamn it, Randall!" Dana tucked Randi under one arm and grabbed his arm hard enough to hurt with her free hand, almost dragging him off his feet. "What part of *run* don't you understand?"

The scale of it didn't really sink in until he saw how fast the whole team was hustling.

They were sprinting hard and he had to kick hard to keep up. But they weren't running for the nearest exit.

Instead, they were hesitating, one at each door, to make sure everyone was out.

He could see that carrying Randi was slowing Dana down from what she needed to do, so he took the Corgi and concentrated on racing to his kitchens at the end of the corridor. The others were moving so fast that they caught up with him when he foolishly hesitated.

No one in the kitchen, but there were eggs scorching on the griddle, water on the boil, a giant motorized whisk beating together another batch of pancake batter.

"Main gas and electric shutoff?" Dana shouted at him.

He pointed and one of the techs yanked the lever.

Out the far end, they were the last onto the lawn.

Together they sprinted toward the crowd gathered out on the golf course.

Dana glanced at her watch then yanked him to a stop as she shouted, "Down! Everybody down!"

Five hundred delegates and two hundred workers all dropped to the cool grass.

Dana yanked him down with her, then scooped Randi into her lap and curled her body around the Corgi.

———

RANDALL TRIED TO REMEMBER IT AFTERWARD, BUT IT NEVER quite came clear.

First had come a geyser of water that blew out all of the ground floor windows.

A bolt of flame roared upward.

Then a massive thump.

The few who remained standing were thrown backward by the shock wave.

He'd been sitting and was knocked flat onto his back. Even some of those lying near the front were rolled over once or twice.

Tiny bits and pieces of hotel began raining down from the sky: flash-charred wood chips, the genuine leather covers of crisped hotel portfolios, underwear stuck to a part of someone's suitcase.

When he finally dared look again, fifty feet of the hotel —from the ballroom straight up through the three stories above—had simply vaporized.

16

Like so many others, he often stopped on the front lawn to stare at the missing section of the hotel. In the last week, they'd sealed the two ends. It had taken a second week of clean-up before they'd reopened the much-reduced hotel yesterday. The rebuild would take well into next season.

"Barn burned down. Now I can see the moon." A voice spoke from behind him.

Randall wanted to weep with relief. He didn't dare turn.

"Basho?" he asked, managing to keep his voice casual.

"Mizuta Masahide, but Basho had some part of the haiku. It works better in the original Japanese, of course."

Dana stepped up beside him, with Randi at her feet.

He still couldn't turn to her. Instead, he watched through the gap in the hotel. The hillsides had peaked with their fall colors and now shed their leaves. The slopes of Mount Washington were now bare-branch brown and conifer green. Soon the snow would come down the slopes and turn the world white and clean for a while.

It was strange, yet oddly perfect to see the mountain *through* the hotel, or where that section of it had been.

"Did you catch him?"

Out of his peripheral vision, he could see the nod by the movement of her fairy-dark hair. "Not me, but yes. Trying to board a plane to the Far East. He was paid to destroy the new monetary plan by a power that enjoys manipulating global currency as a weapon. Of course there's no way to pin it on China, but that's where it came from. The global markets are exacting massive retribution."

"You saved so many lives." Randall couldn't begin to count the cost in lives if Randi and Dana had been one bit less skilled. There'd been plenty of glass cuts and some broken bones, but no death.

"We did." Again that nod, this time toward her dog.

They stood in silence long past when he should be checking up on the start of breakfast service. Long enough for the late autumn dawn to finish lighting the mountain and to start lighting the land.

"I received an offer." Again that fairy whisper.

And again he closed his eyes and prayed to any deity that might be listening. He kept his mouth closed too because he didn't trust what might come out if he opened it.

"Yes."

He finally turned to look at Dana. "Yes? Just yes?"

"Isn't that sufficient?"

"Sufficient?" Randall wanted to shout to the skies. He wanted to hug her. And dance. And... He didn't know what, so he did his best to be calm about it. "Yes, it is."

"It sounds interesting."

At his suggestion, the hotel had offered her two combined positions: a replacement for the Activities and

Athletics Director, and the newly created Security Director. At many times her Secret Service salary.

"There's only one problem."

He swallowed hard and watched her face. No hint of a smile, but those fairy blue eyes were definitely amused.

"The key card you gave me doesn't seem to work." She held up the card he'd given her before the conference had begun. "Do you know where I can get a replacement?"

His room, the room they'd shared, had disappeared in the explosion. Clean slate. Both his belongings and her travel pack were gone.

"I'll," he swallowed hard again but couldn't seem to clear his throat. They'd be together. And she wanted to find that future—with him. "I'll get you a new card."

As he slipped his hand into hers, Randi lay down across his shoe. Tully would enjoy the company.

Randall now understood his parents. With Dana at his side, he could be very content here—it already had everything he needed.

He looked back at the mountain showing through the gap in the hotel.

Yes, very content.

———

*If you enjoyed this book,
please consider leaving a review.
They really help.*

Keep reading for an exciting excerpt from:
White House Protection Force #1: *Off the Leash*

OFF THE LEASH (EXCERPT)

IF YOU ENJOYED THAT, YOU'LL LOVE THE
NOVELS!

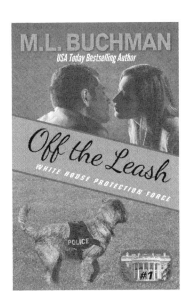

OFF THE LEASH (EXCERPT)

"YOU'RE JOKING."

"Nope. That's his name. And he's yours now."

Sergeant Linda Hamlin wondered quite what it would take to wipe that smile off Lieutenant Jurgen's face. A 120mm round from an MIA1 Abrams Main Battle Tank came to mind.

The kennel master of the US Secret Service's Canine Team was clearly a misogynistic jerk from the top of his polished head to the bottoms of his equally polished boots. She wondered if the shoelaces were polished as well.

Then she looked over at the poor dog sitting hopefully on the concrete kennel floor. His stall had a dog bed three times his size and a water bowl deep enough for him to bathe in. No toys, because toys always came from the handler as a reward. He offered her a sad sigh and a liquid doggy gaze. The kennel even smelled wrong, more of sanitizer than dog. The walls seemed to echo with each bark down the long line of kennels housing the candidate hopefuls for the next addition to the Secret Service's team.

Thor—really?—was a brindle-colored mutt, part who-knew and part no-one-cared. He looked like a cross between an oversized, long-haired schnauzer and a dust mop that someone had spilled dark gray paint on. After mixing in streaks of tawny brown, they'd left one white paw just to make him all the more laughable.

And of course Lieutenant Jerk Jurgen would assign Thor to the first woman on the USSS K-9 team.

Unable to resist, she leaned over far enough to scruff the dog's ears. He was the physical opposite of the sleek and powerful Malinois MWDs—military war dogs—that she'd been handling for the 75th Rangers for the last five years. They twitched with eagerness and nerves. A good MWD was seventy pounds of pure drive—every damn second of the day. If the mild-mannered Thor weighed thirty pounds, she'd be surprised. And he looked like a little girl's best friend who should have a pink bow on his collar.

Jurgen was clearly ex-Marine and would have no respect for the Army. Of course, having been in the Army's Special Operations Forces, she knew better than to respect a Marine.

"We won't let any old swabbie bother us, will we?"

Jurgen snarled—definitely Marine Corps. Swabbie was slang for a Navy sailor and a Marine always took offense at being lumped in with them no matter how much they belonged. Of course the swabbies took offense at having the Marines lumped with *them.* Too bad there weren't any Navy around so that she could get two for the price of one. Jurgen wouldn't be her boss, so appeasing him wasn't high on her to-do list.

At least she wouldn't need any of the protective bite gear working with Thor. With his stature, he was an explosives detection dog without also being an attack one.

"Where was he trained?" She stood back up to face the beast.

"Private outfit in Montana—some place called Henderson's Ranch. Didn't make their MWD program," his scoff said exactly what he thought the likelihood of any dog outfit in Montana being worthwhile. "They wanted us to try the little runt out."

She'd never heard of a training program in Montana. MWDs all came out of Lackland Air Force Base training. The Secret Service mostly trained their own and they all came from Vohne Liche Kennels in Indiana. Unless… Special Operations Forces dogs were trained by private contractors. She'd worked beside a Delta Force dog for a single month—he'd been incredible.

"Is he trained in English or German?" Most American MWDs were trained in German so that there was no confusion in case a command word happened to be part of a spoken sentence. It also made it harder for any random person on the battlefield to shout something that would confuse the dog.

"German according to his paperwork, but he won't listen to me much in either language."

Might as well give the diminutive Thor a few basic tests. A snap of her fingers and a slap on her thigh had the dog dropping into a smart "heel" position. No need to call out *Fuss—by my foot.*

"*Pass auf!*" *Guard!* She made a pistol with her thumb and forefinger and aimed it at Jurgen as she grabbed her forearm with her other hand—the military hand sign for enemy.

The little dog snarled at Jurgen sharply enough to have him backing out of the kennel. "Goddamn it!"

"*Ruhig.*" *Quiet.* Thor maintained his fierce posture but dropped the snarl.

"*Gute Hund.*" *Good dog,* Linda countered the command.

Thor looked up at her and wagged his tail happily. She tossed him a doggie treat, which he caught midair and crunched happily.

She didn't bother looking up at Jurgen as she knelt once more to check over the little dog. His scruffy fur was so soft that it tickled. Good strength in the jaw, enough to show he'd had bite training despite his size—perfect if she ever needed to take down a three-foot-tall terrorist. Legs said he was a jumper.

"Take your time, Hamlin. I've got nothing else to do with the rest of my goddamn day except babysit you and this mutt."

"Is the course set?"

"Sure. Take him out," Jurgen's snarl sounded almost as nasty as Thor's before he stalked off.

She stood and slapped a hand on her opposite shoulder.

Thor sprang aloft as if he was attached to springs and she caught him easily. He'd cleared well over double his own height. Definitely trained...and far easier to catch than seventy pounds of hyperactive Malinois.

She plopped him back down on the ground. On lead or off? She'd give him the benefit of the doubt and try off first to see what happened.

Linda zipped up her brand-new USSS jacket against the cold and led the way out of the kennel into the hard sunlight of the January morning. Snow had brushed the higher hills around the USSS James J. Rowley Training Center—which this close to Washington, DC, wasn't saying much—but was melting quickly. Scents wouldn't carry as well on the cool air, making it more of a challenge for Thor to locate the explosives. She didn't know where they were either. The course was a test for handler as well as dog.

Jurgen would be up in the observer turret looking for any excuse to mark down his newest team. Perhaps teasing him about being just a Marine hadn't been her best tactical choice. She sighed. At least she was consistent—she'd always been good at finding ways to piss people off before she could stop herself and consider the wisdom of doing so.

This test was the culmination of a crazy three months, so she'd forgive herself this time—something she also wasn't very good at.

In October she'd been out of the Army and unsure what to do next. Tucked in the packet with her DD 214 honorable discharge form had been a flyer on career opportunities with the US Secret Service dog team: *Be all your dog can be!* No one else being released from Fort Benning that day had received any kind of a job flyer at all that she'd seen, so she kept quiet about it.

She had to pass through DC on her way back to Vermont—her parent's place. Burlington would work for, honestly, not very long at all, but she lacked anywhere else to go after a decade of service. So, she'd stopped off in DC to see what was up with that job flyer. Five interviews and three months to complete a standard six-month training course later—which was mostly a cakewalk after fighting with the US Rangers—she was on-board and this chill January day was her first chance with a dog. First chance to prove that she still had it. First chance to prove that she hadn't made a mistake in deciding that she'd seen enough bloodshed and war zones for one lifetime and leaving the Army.

The Start Here sign made it obvious where to begin, but she didn't dare hesitate to take in her surroundings past a quick glimpse. Jurgen's score would count a great deal toward where she and Thor were assigned in the future.

Mostly likely on some field prep team, clearing the way for presidential visits.

As usual, hindsight informed her that harassing the lieutenant hadn't been an optimal strategy. A hindsight that had served her equally poorly with regular Army commanders before she'd finally hooked up with the Rangers—kowtowing to officers had never been one of her strengths.

Thankfully, the Special Operations Forces hadn't given a damn about anything except performance and *that* she could always deliver, since the day she'd been named the team captain for both soccer and volleyball. She was never popular, but both teams had made all-state her last two years in school.

The canine training course at James J. Rowley was a two-acre lot. A hard-packed path of tramped-down dirt led through the brown grass. It followed a predictable pattern from the gate to a junker car, over to tool shed, then a truck, and so on into a compressed version of an intersection in a small town. Beyond it ran an urban street of gray clapboard two- and three-story buildings and an eight-story office tower, all without windows. Clearly a playground for Secret Service training teams.

Her target was the town, so she blocked the city street out of her mind. Focus on the problem: two roads, twenty storefronts, six houses, vehicles, pedestrians.

It might look normal...normalish with its missing windows and no movement. It would be anything but. Stocked with fake IEDs, a bombmaker's stash, suicide cars, weapons caches, and dozens of other traps, all waiting for her and Thor to find. He had to be sensitive to hundreds of scents and it was her job to guide him so that he didn't miss the opportunity to find and evaluate each one.

There would be easy scents, from fertilizer and diesel fuel used so destructively in the 1995 Oklahoma City bombing, to almost as obvious TNT to the very difficult to detect C-4 plastic explosive.

Mannequins on the street carried grocery bags and briefcases. Some held fresh meat, a powerful smell demanding any dog's attention, but would count as a false lead if they went for it. On the job, an explosives detection dog wasn't supposed to care about anything except explosives. Other mannequins were wrapped in suicide vests loaded with Semtex or wearing knapsacks filled with package bombs made from Russian PVV-5A.

She spotted Jurgen stepping into a glassed-in observer turret atop the corner drugstore. Someone else was already there and watching.

She looked down once more at the ridiculous little dog and could only hope for the best.

"Thor?"

He looked up at her.

She pointed to the left, away from the beaten path.

"*Such!*" *Find.*

Thor sniffed left, then right. Then he headed forward quickly in the direction she pointed.

————

CLIVE ANDREWS SAT IN THE SECOND-STORY WINDOW AT THE corner of Main and First, the only two streets in town. Downstairs was a drugstore all rigged to explode, except there were no triggers and there was barely enough explosive to blow up a candy box.

Not that he'd know, but that's what Lieutenant Jurgen had promised him.

It didn't really matter if it was rigged to blow for real, because when Miss Watson—never Ms. or Mrs.—asked for a "favor," you did it. At least he did. Actually, he had yet to meet anyone else who knew her. Not that he'd asked around. She wasn't the sort of person one talked about with strangers, or even close friends. He'd bet even if they did, it would be in whispers. That's just what she was like.

So he'd traveled across town from the White House and into Maryland on a cold winter's morning, barely past a sunrise that did nothing to warm the day. Now he sat in an unheated glass icebox and watched a new officer run a test course he didn't begin to understand. Lieutenant Jurgen settled in beside him at a console with feeds from a dozen cameras and banks of switches.

While waiting, Clive had been fooling around with a sketch on a small pad of paper. The next State Dinner was in seven days. President Zachary Taylor had invited the leaders of Vietnam, Japan, and the Philippines to the White House for discussions about some Chinese islands. Or something like that, Clive hadn't really been paying attention to the details past the attendee list.

Instead, he was contemplating the dessert for such a dinner that would surprise, perhaps delight, as well as being an icebreaker for future discussions. Being the chocolatier for the White House was the most exciting job he'd ever had. Every challenge was fresh and new, like the first strawberry of each year.

This one would be elegant. January was a little early, it would be better if it was spring, but that wasn't crucial. A large half-egg shape of paper-thin white chocolate filled with a mousse—white chocolate? No, nor a dark chocolate. Instead, a milk chocolate mousse but rich with flavor, perhaps bourbon. Then mold the dark chocolate to top it with a filigree bird, wings spread in half flight, ready to soar upward. A crane perhaps? He made a note to check with the protocol office to make sure that he wouldn't be offending some leader without knowing it.

"Never underestimate the power of a good dessert," he mumbled one of Jacques Torres' favorite admonitions. This was going to work very nicely.

"What's that?" Jurgen grunted out without looking up.

"Just talking to myself."

Which earned him a dismissive grunt, as if he was unworthy of the agent's attention. It wouldn't surprise him.

———

Keep reading now!
Available at fine retailers everywhere.
Off the Leash

ABOUT THE AUTHOR

USA Today and Amazon #1 Bestseller M. L. "Matt" Buchman began writing on a flight from Japan to ride his bicycle across the Australian Outback. Just part of a solo around-the-world trip that ultimately launched his writing career.

From the very beginning, his powerful female heroines insisted on putting character first, *then* a great adventure. He's since written over 70 action-adventure thrillers and military romantic suspense novels. And just for the fun of it: 100 short stories, and a fast-growing pile of read-by-author audiobooks.

Booklist says: "3X Top 10 of the Year." PW says: "Tom Clancy fans open to a strong female lead will clamor for more." His fans say: "I want more now...of everything." That his characters are even more insistent than his fans is a hoot.

As a 30-year project manager with a geophysics degree who has designed and built houses, flown and jumped out of planes, and solo-sailed a 50' ketch, he is awed by what is possible. More at: www.mlbuchman.com.

Other works by M. L. Buchman: *(* - also in audio)*

Action-Adventure Thrillers

Dead Chef
One Chef!
Two Chef!

Miranda Chase
*Drone**
*Thunderbolt**
*Condor**
*Ghostrider**
*Raider**
*Chinook**
*Havoc**
*White Top**
*Start the Chase**

Science Fiction / Fantasy

Deities Anonymous
Cookbook from Hell: Reheated
Saviors 101

Single Titles
Monk's Maze
the Me and Elsie Chronicles

Contemporary Romance

Eagle Cove
Return to Eagle Cove
Recipe for Eagle Cove
Longing for Eagle Cove
Keepsake for Eagle Cove

Love Abroad
Heart of the Cotswolds: England
Path of Love: Cinque Terre, Italy

Where Dreams
Where Dreams are Born
Where Dreams Reside
*Where Dreams Are of Christmas**
Where Dreams Unfold
Where Dreams Are Written
Where Dreams Continue

Non-Fiction

Strategies for Success
Managing Your Inner Artist/Writer
*Estate Planning for Authors**
Character Voice
Narrate and Record Your Own
*Audiobook**

Short Story Series by M. L. Buchman:

Action-Adventure Thrillers

Dead Chef

Miranda Chase Origin Stories

Romantic Suspense

Antarctic Ice Fliers

US Coast Guard

Contemporary Romance

Eagle Cove

Other

Deities Anonymous (fantasy)

Single Titles

The Emily Beale Universe
(military romantic suspense)

The Night Stalkers
MAIN FLIGHT
The Night Is Mine
I Own the Dawn
Wait Until Dark
Take Over at Midnight
Light Up the Night
Bring On the Dusk
By Break of Day
Target of the Heart
Target Lock on Love
Target of Mine
Target of One's Own
NIGHT STALKER HOLIDAYS
*Daniel's Christmas**
*Frank's Independence Day**
*Peter's Christmas**
Christmas at Steel Beach
*Zachary's Christmas**
*Roy's Independence Day**
*Damien's Christmas**
Christmas at Peleliu Cove

Henderson's Ranch
*Nathan's Big Sky**
*Big Sky, Loyal Heart**
*Big Sky Dog Whisperer**
*Tales of Henderson's Ranch**

Shadow Force: Psi
*At the Slightest Sound**
*At the Quietest Word**
*At the Merest Glance**
*At the Clearest Sensation**

Dilya's Dog Force
(formerly:
White House Protection Force)
*Off the Leash**
*On Your Mark**
*In the Weeds**

Firehawks
Pure Heat
Full Blaze
*Hot Point**
*Flash of Fire**
Wild Fire
SMOKEJUMPERS
*Wildfire at Dawn**
*Wildfire at Larch Creek**
*Wildfire on the Skagit**

Delta Force
*Target Engaged**
*Heart Strike**
*Wild Justice**
*Midnight Trust**

Emily Beale Universe Short Story Series

The Night Stalkers
The Night Stalkers Stories
The Night Stalkers CSAR
The Night Stalkers Wedding Stories
The Future Night Stalkers

Delta Force
Th Delta Force Shooters
The Delta Force Warriors

Firehawks
The Firehawks Lookouts
The Firehawks Hotshots
The Firebirds

Dilya's Dog Force
Stories

Future Night Stalkers
Stories (Science Fiction)

The Emily Beale Universe
Reading Order Road Map

any series and any novel may be read stand-alone
(all have a complete heartwarming happy ever after)

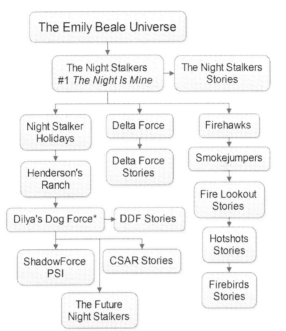

The Emily Beale Universe

↓

The Night Stalkers
#1 *The Night Is Mine* → The Night Stalkers Stories

↓

Night Stalker Holidays	Delta Force	Firehawks
↓	↓	↓
Henderson's Ranch	Delta Force Stories	Smokejumpers
↓		↓
Dilya's Dog Force* → DDF Stories		Fire Lookout Stories
↓		↓
ShadowForce PSI CSAR Stories		Hotshots Stories
↓		↓
The Future Night Stalkers		Firebirds Stories

* *Formerly:* White House Protection Force
For more information and alternate reading orders, please visit:
www.mlbuchman.com/reading-order

SIGN UP FOR M. L. BUCHMAN'S NEWSLETTER TODAY

and receive:
Release News
Free Short Stories
a Free Book

Get your free book today. Do it now.
free-book.mlbuchman.com

Printed in Great Britain
by Amazon